Jesus' Birthday Wish

By Yolanda Villafana

Illustrated by Deborah Delaney

Share the Good News
of Jesus where ever
you go.
Yolda Villafana
2018

This book is dedicated to our LORD and Savior, Jesus Christ.

For God So loved the world that He gave His only Son, that whoever believes in Him will not perish but have everlasting life. John 3:16

Did you know that Christmas

is Jesus' birthday?

He is over 2000 years old!

That is a lot of birthdays.

And a lot of birthday wishes.

If Jesus could have a birthday wish, what do you think that wish would be? Would He wish for a birthday cake?

Or a Jolly Jump?

Or maybe a present underneath the Christmas tree?

Jesus watches us from above, rushing to and fro.

Busy, busy at Christmas time, so much to do and too many places to go.

We hang our lights.

We put a star on the tree.

Santa makes his appearance.

In him, the children believe and

are eager to see.

But, the Birthday Boy,

the guest of honor,

He is nowhere to be found.

While we all play, laugh, and

cheer, I think Jesus may shed a

little tear.

If Jesus told us His
birthday wish,
I think that it would
simply be...

"When you celebrate Christmas with your family, can you please remember to include Me?"

"I don't need a fancy house
or lots of stuff underneath
the tree.
I don't need holiday decorations
for all the world to see."

"I don't even need an expensive Nativity.
All I want is to be invited to My own birthday party."

"My only wish, My Child, is for you to delight in Me and seek Me first in all you say and do. And, I promise as your LORD and SAVIOR, all your heavenly wishes will come true."

Delight yourself in the LORD,
and He shall give you the desires of your heart.
Seek first the kingdom of God and His righteousness,
and all these things shall be added to you.
(Psalm 37:4; Matthew 6:33 NKJV)

About this book:

What are "heavenly wishes?" Are they wishes for more toys, fancy cars, or more money? No. Those are earthly wishes. What the Bible says is that the more we get to know God, the more our wishes will reflect God's heart. How does one get to know God's heart? By receiving and believing in His Son, Jesus, and reading God's love letter to us which is the Bible. If you'd like to receive Jesus in your heart as LORD and Savior, here is a simple prayer you can pray:

Dear Jesus,

Please forgive me of my sins. Thank you for dying on the cross for me. I believe You rose from the dead and are now seated in heaven with God, the Father. I invite You to come live in my heart as my LORD and Savior. Fill me with Your Holy Spirit and help me to live my life for You. In Jesus Name I pray. Amen.

Also available:

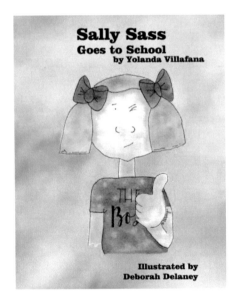

Coming soon in Spring 2019

Bea Kind Meets Grumpy Gilbert

30394411R00018